UNDER-THE-BED FRED

Linda Bailey

Illustrated by Colin Jack

tundra

Tundra Books, an imprint of Penguin Random House Canada
Young Readers, a Penguin Random House Company

Library and Archives Canada Cataloguing in Publication

Bailey, Linda, 1948-, author
Under-the-bed Fred / by Linda Bailey ; illustrated by Colin Jack.

Issued in print and electronic formats.
ISBN 978-1-77049-553-1 (bound).—ISBN 978-1-77049-555-5 (epub)

I. Jack, Colin, illustrator II. Title.

PS8553.A3644U54 2016 jC813'.54 C2015-904006-X

Published simultaneously in the United States of America by Tundra Books of Northern New York, an imprint of Penguin Random House Canada Young Readers, a Penguin Random House Company

Library of Congress Control Number: 2015947654

Edited by Tara Walker and Jessica Burgess
Designed by Terri Nimmo
The artwork in this book was rendered in Photoshop.
The text was set in ITC Stone.
Printed and bound in China

www.penguinrandomhouse.ca

1 2 3 4 5 21 20 19 18 17

Penguin Random House
TUNDRA BOOKS

TO MY WONDERFUL PAL
IN BOOKS AND IN WRITING,
DEBORAH HODGE

LB

FOR GABRIEL AND ELI

CJ

Chapter 1

Leo Meets the Monster

There was a monster under Leo's bed.

Leo could hear it at night. Sometimes it growled. Sometimes it creaked. Once it let out a horrible moan.

ALIEN

The monster was a huge problem. Especially at bedtime. Leo had to leap all the way from the door to the bed so the monster wouldn't grab his ankles.

And then he was *stuck* there! The monster kept Leo trapped in his bed all night long. Sometimes Leo had to go to the bathroom really badly. But he knew the monster was waiting.

One night, Leo really, REALLY had to go. He took a deep breath.

"Hey, you!" he said.

The monster stopped growling. "You mean me?"

"Yes," said Leo. "You."

"Oh!" said the monster, sounding surprised.

"I need to go to the bathroom," said Leo.

A long time passed.

"Do you want me to come with you?" asked the monster.

"NO!" said Leo.

"Well, what do you want?"

"Nothing," said Leo. "Just stay there. Don't move. Do nothing."

"Okay," said the monster.

CHOMPERS
Star Battles

Leo couldn't believe it was so easy. He got out of bed and walked to the bathroom. Nobody grabbed his ankles.

He walked back. Nobody grabbed his ankles again.

"Wow!" thought Leo as he got into bed.

"Was that okay?" asked the monster.

"That was fine," said Leo.

“Well,” said the monster, “goodnight then.”

“Goodnight,” said Leo. “Don’t let the bedbugs bite.”

“Bugs?” said the monster. “There are bugs here?”

“No,” said Leo. “No bugs. Go to sleep.”

“Okay,” said the monster.

A long time passed.

"Are you *sure* about the bugs?" asked the monster.

"I'm sure," said Leo. "Go to sleep."

If you happen
to have more
Dinosaurs
GRRRRRROWWLL!
CREEEEAAAAK!
MOOOAAAANNN!

Chapter 2

The Monster Gets a Name

Leo had solved his monster problem. He could get into bed. He could get out of bed. In. Out. In. Out. His ankles were safe!

But the monster was still there. Growl. Creak. Moan. Leo could *hear* him in the night.

So Leo got more and more curious.

Finally, he couldn't stand it anymore.

"Hey, you!" he said.

"Me?" said the monster.

"Yes. You. I was just wondering. Why are you under my bed?"

"Oh," said the monster. "I live here."

Leo pulled his covers up to his chin.

"How long have you been there?" he asked.

"I don't know," said the monster. "I came with the bed."

Leo took a deep breath. Then he asked a very brave question.

"Can you come out?"

The monster didn't answer.

He didn't have to.

Leo's bed started to rise.

It rocked to one side.

It rolled to the other.

Leo grabbed his mattress.

He held on so tight, his fingers hurt.

Groan. Creak. Moan.

CREEEEAAAAK!
GRRRRRROAN!
MOOOAAAANNN!

"Hi!" said the monster.

Leo looked up. The monster was ENORMOUS!

"Hi," said Leo in a teeny, tiny voice.

He stared.

The monster stared back.

Nobody moved.

“Do you mind if I sit down?” asked the monster.

“Good idea,” said Leo.

OLD
EYE
It CAME from
DOWN Below
Killer

The monster sat on the floor. He looked much better there.

"What's your name?" asked Leo.

"I don't have one," said the monster.

"Everyone should have a name," said Leo.

"I know," said the monster. "I like Fred."

Leo blinked. "You want to be called Fred?"

"Could I?"

"I don't see why not," said Leo.

"Then say it," said the monster. "Say Fred. Say it nicely."

"Okay," said Leo. "Hi Fred. How are you doing, Fred? How's life, Fred?"

"Oh," said Fred. "That feels *good*!"

"Fred's a good name," said Leo. "Easy to say. Easy to spell, too."

"What's spell?" said Fred.

Leo found a piece of paper. He wrote "Fred" on the paper in big letters.

"That's you," he said. "Fred."

Then he drew a picture.

"See?" said Leo. "There's my bed. And there's you. Under the bed. Fred."

He gave Fred the paper.

"For me?" said Fred. "Oh, thank you, Leo. Thank you."

"That's okay," said Leo.

"Everyone should have a name."

Leo got back in his bed. Fred crawled underneath.

"Fred," said Fred. "Fred, Fred, Fred, Fred, Fred."

"Goodnight," said Leo.

"Fred, Fred, Fred," said Fred.

"Are you going to keep doing that?" asked Leo.

"Fred, Fred, Fred."

"Oh, for Pete's sake," said Leo. He rolled over. He put his pillow over his head.

"Fred, Fred, Fred, Fred, Fred . . ." said Fred.

Fred

Fred

Fred

Fred

Fred

Chapter 3

Fred Shows His Stuff

"I'm tired of being under the bed," said Fred. "There's nothing to do."

"Nothing?" said Leo.

"Well, just one thing," said Fred.

"What's that?" asked Leo.

"Scare you," said Fred.

"That's all you get to do?" said Leo. "Ever?"

"Yes," said Fred. "It's my job."

"But I'm not scared of you anymore," said Leo.

“Yes, you are,” said Fred.

“No, I’m not,” said Leo. “You’re not that scary.”

“Yes, I am,” said Fred. “Watch THIS!”

In a wink, Fred
became . . . a huge hairy
LION! The lion let out a
roar that shook the lightbulbs.

Leo flew backward till he hit the wall.
"Yeeks!" he yelled.

The lion stretched out and became . . .
a king cobra SNAKE!

Leo could see its fangs.
He slid to the floor.
"Help!" he whispered.

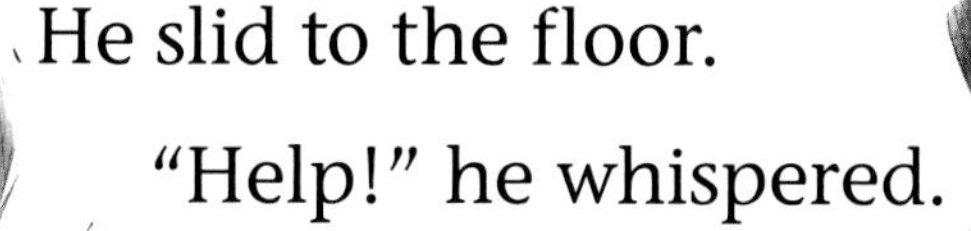

The snake grew even bigger and became . . . a fire-breathing DRAGON! It had yellow eyes. It had teeth as sharp as knives.

And it was coming for Leo!

Leo covered his face with both hands. He made funny little sounds like this. "Nuh. Nuh. Nuh. Nuh. Nuh."

"Are you okay?" asked Fred.

Leo opened his eyes.

"Did I scare you?" asked Fred.

Leo didn't answer. He couldn't. He was still saying, "Nuh. Nuh. Nuh."

Fred asked again, "Did I scare you?"

"A little," said Leo. "Yes, that was a bit scary."

“Sorry,” said Fred. “I *have* to scare you. It’s my job.”

“I know,” said Leo.

Leo got into bed. Fred got under the bed. Leo turned out the light.

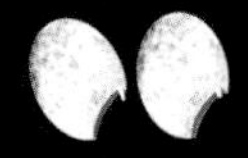

“Fred?” said Leo in the dark.

“Yes?” said Fred.

“You’re very good at your job.”

“Thank you,” said Fred. “Goodnight.”

“Sleep tight,” said Leo. “Don’t let the bedbugs bite.”

“Bugs?” said Fred. “There are bugs?”

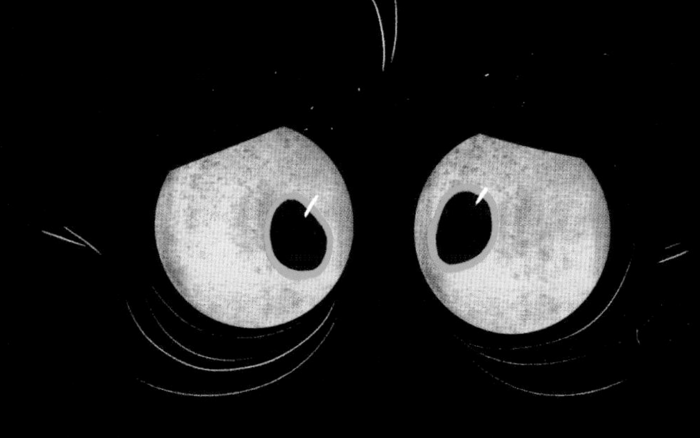

Chapter 4

Sam the Man

One day some visitors came. Mrs. Bing and her son, Sam. Sam was one year older than Leo.

Leo's mom smiled. "Do you like grape juice?" she asked Sam.

"I love grape juice," said Sam. "Thank you."

Leo's mom poured two glasses of grape juice. She told the boys to go play in Leo's room.

"Play nice," said Sam's mom.

Sam didn't like to play nice. There was only one game that Sam liked to play. Gimmee.

"Gimmee that truck," said Sam. SMASH went the truck.

"Gimmee that space station," said Sam.

CRASH went the space station.

"I'm Sam the Man," said Sam. "Say it."

"If that's what you want," said Leo. "You're Sam the Man."

"Gimmee your shoe," said Sam.

"My shoe?" said Leo. "I need my shoe."

"Gimmee," said Sam.

Leo gave him the shoe. Sam filled it with grape juice.

"What are you boys doing?" called the moms.

"Nothing!" yelled Sam.

"Gimmee your other shoe," said Sam. "I still have some more grape juice."

Leo took off his other shoe. He threw it under the bed.

"Oops!" he said.

"Why did you do that?" said Sam. "Now I have to fill your shoe with spit." He crawled under the bed to get it.

A moment later, Sam let out a yell. "YIKES! There's something under here!"

"Sam the Man," said Leo, "meet Fred the Monster."

"What are you boys doing?" called the moms.

"Nothing!" yelled Leo.

When Sam finally came out, he was holding Leo's shoe.

"Here," he said. "It's okay. There's no spit in it. I have to go now."

From under the bed came a growl.

Sam jumped. "Oh," he said. "I forgot! Sorry! I have to say sorry."

Another growl. Louder.

"I am very sorry, Leo, for pouring juice in your shoe," said Sam. "I am so sorry. I am the most sorry person ever in the whole world. Can I go now? Please?"

GRRR!

"Sure," said Leo. "Go."

Sam ran out. When he passed the bed, he did a giant leap. But nobody grabbed his ankles.

"Hey, Fred?" said Leo.

"What?"

"Thank you," said Leo.

"That's okay," said Fred. "It's my job."

Chapter 5

Fred Goes to School

Every day Leo went to school. Every day he came home and told Fred all about it.

One day Leo said, "Tomorrow we're having show and tell."

"What's show and tell?" said Fred.

"We have to take something interesting to school," said Leo. "To show the other kids. I never have anything good to show."

"That's sad," said Fred.

"Yes," said Leo. "It is."

“You could take your soccer ball,” said Fred.

“Not interesting,” said Leo.

“You could take a banana. You like bananas.”

“I like them,” said Leo. “But they’re not interesting.”

Then Leo had an idea.

"Fred?" he said. "Could I take . . . you?"

"Me?" said Fred. "Am I interesting?"

"Fred," said Leo, "you are the most interesting thing in this house. You are the most interesting thing in this city. You are the most interesting thing I have ever *seen*!"

“Me?” said Fred. “Really?”

“You,” said Leo. “Really.”

“Okay,” said Fred. “You can show me at school.”

IF YOU happen
to have more
DINOSAURS
9:00
KNOCK!
KNOCK!
KNOCK!

Late that night, Fred knocked on the bottom of the bed.

"Yes?" said Leo.

"I won't know anybody at school," said Fred.

"You know me," said Leo.

"That's true," said Fred. "I know you very well. BOO!"

"Cut that out," said Leo.

The next day Leo and Fred walked to school together. Fred wore Leo's father's overcoat.

When they got there, Leo told the teacher, "He's my show and tell."

"Oh, my goodness," said the teacher.

"Where can he sit?" asked Leo.

"At the back," said the teacher. "At the very, very back."

Fred sat down. A fly flew in. It flew past Fred.

"BOO!" said Fred to the fly.

Everyone turned to look.

"I can't help it," said Fred. "It's my job."

Soon it was time for show and tell. Max showed his magic set. Lilly showed her paints.

Finally it was Leo's turn. "This is Fred," he said.

HANGIN there
This is Fred
MS. Gondwana

All the kids stared at Fred.

"What's a Fred?" they asked. "Is he a pet? A toy?"

"He's my monster," said Leo. "He lives under my bed."

"You call that a monster?" said David. "He's not scary. I have a monster in *my* closet, and he's really scary."

"Have you seen your monster?" asked Leo.

"No," said David. "But I know he's there."

"Maybe he's shy," said Fred. "I used to be shy."

"Shy?" said David. "Ha ha ha. This monster is *not* scary."

"Yes, I am," said Fred. "Watch THIS!"

And before Leo could stop him, Fred turned into . . . a huge hairy LION!

Then he turned into . . . a king cobra SNAKE!

Then he turned into . . . a fire-breathing

DRAGON!

"Nuh," said David. "Nuh. Nuh. Nuh."

When the dragon came closer, David stopped saying “Nuh.” He ran out of the room. So did all the other kids. So did the teacher.

Leo and Fred were alone.

"That was fun," said Fred.

"Oh, Fred," said Leo, shaking his head. "Fred, Fred, Fred."

Fred and Leo walked home together.

"I LOVE school," said Fred. "I love, love, love it. I can't wait to go back. When can I go back?"

"Well," said Leo, "maybe not right away."

Fred stopped walking. "I was hoping tomorrow," he said.

"Don't worry," said Leo. "We can have our own school at home."

"Can we?"

"Yes!" said Leo. "No problem."

"Oh, goody," said Fred. "Let's start now!"

And they did.